Special thanks to
Emily Sharratt

Reading Consultant: Prue Goodwin, lecturer in literacy and children's books.

ORCHARD BOOKS

First published in 2018 by The Watts Publishing Group

1 3 5 7 9 10 8 6 4 2

A CIP catalogue record for this book is available from the British Library.

ISBN 978 1 40835 479 7

Printed and bound in China

The paper and board used in this book are made from wood from responsible sources.

Orchard Books
An imprint of Hachette Children's Group
Part of The Watts Publishing Group Limited
Carmelite House, 50 Victoria Embankment, London EC4Y 0DZ

An Hachette UK Company
www.hachette.co.uk
www.hachettechildrens.co.uk

THE LITTEN MYSTERY

ORCHARD

MEET ASH AND PIKACHU!

ASH

A Pokémon dreamer who wants to have it all – including becoming a Pokémon Master!

PIKACHU

Ash's first partner Pokémon and long-time companion!

LOOK OUT FOR THESE POKÉMON

STOUTLAND

LITTEN

ALOLAN PERSIAN

PIKACHU

TOGEDEMARU

CONTENTS

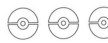

PART ONE: LITTEN ENCOUNTER

PART TWO: RUNAWAY LITTEN

PART THREE: LITTEN'S SECRET

PART ONE
Litten Encounter

CHAPTER ONE

Sandwich Thief

One morning, on Melemele Island in the Alola region, Ash and Pikachu saw a small Pokémon crossing their path.

"Hello," Ash said to the Pokémon.

But the Pokémon just stared back at him.

"That's a Litten," Ash's new Rotom Dex told him. "The Fire Cat Pokémon. A Fire type. Litten show few emotions and prefer to be alone."

As Rotom Dex spoke, Litten approached Ash. It purred and began to rub against Ash's legs.

"It seems pretty friendly to me," Ash said. "Maybe it's hungry." He reached into his bag and pulled out his lunch box.

"Look," Ash said to Litten. "You can have some of my sandwich."

Ash tore a piece off his sandwich and held it out to Litten. But the Pokémon looked at the rest of the sandwich Ash was still holding. It then leaped up and snatched it!

Before he had time to think what he was doing, Ash grabbed the Litten's tail to stop it from running off. At once, the Litten turned around and swiped at Ash with its sharp claws.

"Hey!" Ash protested.

When Rotom Dex chased after the Litten, it gave Rotom Dex a kick, sending it crashing into Pikachu.

Then, while they were still struggling back to their feet, the Litten ran out of sight. It still had the sandwich in its mouth.

CHAPTER TWO

Catch that Litten!

Later, Ash was telling his new friends from the Pokémon School all about his encounter with Litten.

"Ah, so you've met Litten at last!" Mallow said.

"You know Litten?" said Ash.

"It comes to the school all the time, asking for food," Mallow said, nodding. "It's so cute!"

"I can't say no to it!" Lana agreed.

"Humph!" Ash said crossly. "I don't think it's so cute."

"It stole my sandwich!" Ash said.

"Litten's not your average Pokémon," said Sophocles. "They say it can take years to get used to a Trainer."

"Well, someone should teach it not to go around stealing people's food!" said Ash.

"What do you mean?" asked Lillie.

Ash thought for a moment. "I know what to do!" he declared. "I'll catch it!"

Later that day, Ash was walking through the market with Professor Kukui. He was his teacher and guide in Alola.

"We've just got a few things left to buy and then we're finished," Professor Kukui was saying.

Just then, Ash spotted Litten running past.

"Hey, wait!" he cried, sprinting after it.

Ash soon lost Litten among the stalls.

"Would you like to buy some berries, dear?" asked a kindly market seller.

"No, thank you," said Ash. "I was just looking for someone. Hey!" he said suddenly.

Litten was eating berries at the woman's feet.

CHAPTER THREE

Litten and Persian

Litten growled at Ash, who clenched his fists in response.

"Do you feed that Litten?" he asked the lady.

"Of course," she replied. "I love to feed Litten. It comes to see me every day."

Litten stopped eating. It ran

off and they watched it go.

"I have no idea where Litten lives, but it certainly is a dear."

The next day, Ash, Pikachu and Rotom Dex were walking along the cliffs when they heard a strange noise.

Ash looked over to see Litten facing a large grey Pokémon. Litten was backing away, looking scared, as the bigger Pokémon approached.

"Rotom, what is that Pokémon?" Ash asked.

"It's a Persian," Rotom Dex replied.

"A Persian?" said Ash. "It's not like any Persian I've ever seen before!"

"An Alolan Persian looks different from the kind you are

used to," said Rotom, showing Ash on its screen. "The Alolan Persian is a Dark type," Rotom continued. "It can be cunning with a bit of a mean streak."

Ash narrowed his eyes at the Persian.

It was still moving nearer to Litten. It hissed threateningly. Litten was getting closer and closer to the edge of the cliff.

Suddenly, the Persian swiped at Litten with its claws, sending the smaller Pokémon flying.

"Stop that!" yelled Ash.

PART TWO
Runaway Litten

CHAPTER FOUR
Clifftop Battle

"All this for one berry?" Ash asked the snarling Persian, as Litten licked its wounds. "You're being way too rough!"

The Persian used Power Gem. The gem in the centre of its forehead lit up. It shot a laser beam in Ash's direction. Ash leapt out of the way.

While its enemy had been distracted, Litten had picked up the berry again. It inched away from the cliff edge, but suddenly Persian pounced back in its direction. A shower of rocks crumbled down the cliff edge.

"I said stop it!" shouted Ash. "Pikachu – use Electro Ball!"

At once Pikachu jumped into the air, crackling with energy. It fired an electric charge from its tail.

Persian hopped out of the way and shot another beam from its gem that hit the rock Pikachu was sitting on.

"Use Thunderbolt!" Ash said.

"Pikachu!" yelled Ash's Pokémon, hitting Persian with the full force of Thunderbolt.

Persian yelped and ran away.

"Yes!" said Ash.

Then Ash turned to face Litten. It was hobbling away with the berry still held tightly in its mouth. "Hey, Litten, are you OK?" asked Ash.

"Litten has taken a lot of damage," said Rotom Dex sadly, as Litten dropped the berry wearily.

CHAPTER FIVE

The Pokémon Center

"Here, let me carry your berry," said Ash, reaching out. But Litten turned and bit Ash, before picking up the berry again.

Litten took a few more steps but then stopped, panting.

"That's it," said Ash, "I'm taking you to the Pokémon Center!" He picked Litten up, but the little Pokémon squirmed out of his grip. It dropped to the ground and released a fire ball.

"Litten, come on! We're trying to help you," said Ash.

Litten swayed on its feet, then toppled over. Even then, it kept reaching for the berry.

"I understand," Ash said. "I promise, no one is trying to take the berry."

"But we have to get you to
the Pokémon Center!"

With that, he grabbed
Litten by the scruff of its neck.
He carried it, wriggling and
hissing, towards the Pokémon
Center.

At the Pokémon Center,
Nurse Joy put a collar around
Litten's neck.

"That's to stop it from licking
its wounds," she told Ash.

"Looking good, Litten!" Ash said. Litten growled in response.

"It's your turn now, Ash," Nurse Joy continued. "Litten's not the only one who's injured." She pointed to the scratches covering Ash's arms and face.

Ash laughed, and held his arms out for Nurse Joy.

Before they knew it, Litten had grabbed its berry again and run out the door.

CHAPTER SIX

Sleepover

"Ash," cried Nurse Joy. "You have to make sure Litten doesn't hurt itself again while it's still healing."

"Right!" said Ash, racing after Litten, with Pikachu and Rotom Dex behind him.

Litten tried to escape Ash by jumping through some railings but it had forgotten about its collar. It bounced back from the railings and onto the ground.

Ash picked it up gently. "You have to stop running away!"

"You're only hurting yourself," Ash said.

Ash took Litten back to Professor Kukui's house for the night.

"Pika!" said Pikachu, pointing to Litten who was squirming around on the sofa, trying to get comfortable.

"That collar is in the way," said Ash. "I'll take it off, but you have to promise not to lick your wounds."

Ash reached out and unfastened the collar.

Litten stretched happily. Ash
picked it up and petted it until
it fell asleep.

"Goodnight, Litten," Ash said.

Later that night, Ash woke
to hear Litten scratching at the
door to be let out.

"Yeah, yeah, OK," said Ash,
still half-asleep. "I'll open it."

Litten quickly ran out of the
open door.

The moment Litten had escaped, Ash's eyes popped wide open. "What have I done?" he asked.

PART THREE

Litten's Secret

CHAPTER SEVEN

Stoutland

"Where's Litten going now?"
Ash wailed. He, Pikachu and
Rotom Dex raced after the
small Pokémon through the
dark streets of Melemele Island.

Rotom Dex warned Ash,
"Litten's full recovery requires

lots of sleep and no stress!"

They followed Litten up stairs, round corners and all the way to the edge of the town. Litten ran up the steps to a large and rundown house.

"Where are we?" Ash asked.

"Data incomplete," replied Rotom Dex.

They walked in the door after Litten, and saw it passing the berry to a large, shaggy Pokémon.

When Litten saw them, it turned and started hissing.

"A Stoutland," said Ash, recognising the bigger Pokémon.

"And not a young one, by the looks of things," said Rotom Dex, nodding towards the Stoutland.

"I wonder if Litten's been stealing food to bring to Stoutland," Ash said, approaching slowly.

"Poor Stoutland – its dinner is very late because of me!" Ash said.

"Litten, I hoped to catch you for my team, but now I see that you're needed here, Ash said.

Ash stood up. "We should get going. But I'll come and visit — and bring lots of food!"

Suddenly Litten hissed again.

Stoutland began to growl.

"What is it?" said Ash.

"It seems something is approaching," Rotom Dex replied.

They looked up and saw Persian looking in the window above.

CHAPTER EIGHT

Persian's Revenge

"Persian!" The Pokémon growled, leaping down in front of them. The gem on its head began to glow.

"Quick, let's get outside!" said Ash. They all hurried out, Persian just behind them.

"Persian is here for revenge!"
said Rotom Dex.

Litten turned to face Persian,
hissing and growling. Pikachu
stood with it.

"Be careful!" Ash said.

Persian prowled closer.

"OK," said Ash. "Pikachu, use Thunderbolt!"

Pikachu fired Thunderbolt towards Persian, at the same time as Litten shot another fire ball in its direction.

Persian leapt out of the way of both, and towards Ash.

It swiped viciously at Ash with its claws.

"It'll take more than a few scratches to hurt me!" said Ash, showing his already bandaged arms.

Litten and Persian faced each other once more.

Persian sharpened its claws. Litten used Ember attack, shooting off another fire ball, but Persian simply batted it out of the way.

Litten stood still as it grew the biggest and most powerful fire ball yet.

"Litten!" it cried, as the fire ball hurtled towards Persian, hitting it full force. Persian yowled and ran off, its tail still burning.

"You did it, Litten!" Ash cheered, waving his arms in the air. Ash stopped, wincing in pain.

CHAPTER NINE

Alolan Mysteries

The next day, Ash ran all the way to the big old house. He had two bags bursting with food in his hands.

"Litten!" he shouted, as he ran up the steps into the house. "Litten?"

Ash, Rotom Dex and Pikachu walked through the door, but the house was empty. There was no sign off Litten or Stoutland.

Ash walked sadly back to the market and told the old lady everything.

"It must be my fault," he said, hanging his head.

"It's nobody's fault," said the market seller, peeling one of the berries he had returned with. "Pokémon are different from people, that's all."

She put the berry on a saucer at her feet. "I'm sure Litten's doing just fine."

As she spoke, Litten appeared from behind her and walked up to the saucer.

"Litten!" Ash exclaimed, making the Pokémon jump.

"There now, what did I tell you?" said the old lady. "Litten, I hear you've moved."

"Litten!" agreed the Pokémon.

Litten and Ash stared at each other for a moment. Then Litten grabbed the berry and ran off. Ash watched it go.

He wasn't sure he'd ever understand Litten.

But one thing was for sure. There were many more Pokémon to discover and adventures to be had in Alola.

DON'T MISS THESE OTHER OFFICIAL POKÉMON BOOKS